D0409435

Happy Hooves

Oh! Oh! Oh!

For Barnaby, Oliver, Bertie, Noah & Phoebe.
A.B.

For Jamie and Marion. Happy Christmas! x
R.E.

Lancashire Library Services	
30118129841338	
PETERS	JF
£10.99	26-Dec-2014
NGA	

First published in 2014 by Fat Fox Books ltd

Fox's Den, Wickets, Frittenden Road, Staplehurst, Kent TN12 0DH.
www.fatfoxbooks.com

ISBN: 978-0992872823

Fat Fox and associated logos are trademarks and/or registered
trademarks of Fat Fox Books Ltd.

Text copyright © A. Bogie 2014.
Illustrations copyright © Rebecca Elliott 2014.

The right of A. Bogie to be identified as the author and Rebecca Elliott
to be identified as the illustrator of this work has been asserted.

A CIP catalogue record for this book is available from the British Library.

All rights reserved.

Printed and bound in China.

Happy Hooves
Oh! Oh! Oh!

A. Bogie   Rebecca Elliott

fat fox

fatfoxbooks.com

It was Christmas Eve and snow was falling,
Cow had been singing carols all morning.
Her barn was decked with tinsel and holly,
The festive season made her feel

jolly.

Where were her friends?
The happy hooves bunch,
Cow found them nearby, sleeping off lunch.

'Wake up!' she yelled,
'There's no time to lose,
I can't believe you're having a snooze!'

She shook her head in disbelief.
'Let me explain,' (through gritted teeth),
'You can't be lazy, let's do things right,
Or Santa won't come down the chimney tonight.'

'Now tidy-up, make everything gleam,
Even on top of the dusty old beam.
No crumbs on the floor, no dirt can be seen,
Santa must see how good you've all been.'

The pig swiftly ran to his humble abode,
Wiped off the mud and got rid of a toad.
Evicting a mob of **mischievous slugs,**
He then chased away a family of bugs.

But something was wrong when Pig looked up high...
No chimney for Santa in his sty!
("Ho! Ho! Ho!") 'Is that Santa I hear?

Oh! Oh! Oh!

He must be near!'

The pig was worried, and ran to the sheep,
'Do you have space for
me to sleep?'

'Of course.' Sheep said. 'You're welcome to stay,
But I need to clean up straightaway.'

The sheep ran off to his drafty house,
Opened the door and threw out a mouse.
He dusted the rafters, startled a bat,
Whose **flapping escape**
scared off a rat.

But something was missing above Sheep's head...
No chimney for Santa in his shed!
("Ho! Ho! Ho!") 'Is that Santa I hear?

Oh! Oh! Oh!

He must be near!'

Now Sheep and Pig were in distress
And hoped that Donkey could solve this mess.

'Sleep here with me!' Donkey cried,
'But I must tidy up, it's mucky inside.'

The donkey jogged to his room in the yard,
And hung up his last

Christmas card.

He brushed away the old yellow straw,
A pile of twigs, and an apple core.

But something looked odd on Donkey's wall...
No chimney for Santa in his stall!
("Ho! Ho! Ho!") 'Is that Santa I hear?

Oh! Oh! Oh!

He must be near!'

Pig, Sheep and Donkey were now uptight
So asked the foal for a bed for the night.
'Come in!' Foal said, 'And have forty winks,
Though I must clear these dishes...
something stinks!'

Foal dashed around her cosy shack,
And shooed off the cats who were having a yak,
She washed and swept to clean every spot,
Unearthing the culprit, a

mouldy pot!

But something seemed strange above Foal's table...
No chimney for Santa in her stable!
("Ho! Ho! Ho!") 'Is that Santa I hear?

Oh! Oh! Oh!

He must be near!'

The donkey, the pig, the sheep and the foal,
Raced to the cow, by the waterhole.
'Oh Cow, this news will make you glum,
We've got no chimneys for Santa to come!'

Cow chuckled loudly 'Santa won't care,
He can deliver gifts **anywhere!**

'If your home is a stall, a barn or a shed,
He'll find the stocking by your bed.

If you live in a stable or even a sty,
He'll always come if you leave a mince pie!
But now you are here, have Christmas with me,
Lets spend it together

around the Tree.

It's cold outside, come in from the snow,
I hear Santa laughing Ho! Ho! Ho!

We've all been good, so he'll find a way
To deliver our presents on Christmas Day!'